A FARM PREPARES FOR WINTER

SLEEP TIGHT FARM

By Eugenie Doyle Illustrated by Becca Stadtlander

chronicle books · san francisco

The December days shorten and darken.

We are busy
    putting the farm to bed.

With our crops mostly in—strawberries, raspberries,

vegetables, honey, and hay—

now is the time to prepare for deep frost, the coming wind and snow.

Many hands make work light, Mom says.

We shake straw over berry plants
to blanket them from winter's frosty bite.
Next April and May they'll leaf out green
and blossom white.
In June they'll give fruit
so red and juicy we'll make jam and freeze berries
to eat till summer comes again.
We lick our lips,
remembering.

*Good night, strawberries,
covered with straw.*

We cut kale and chard and broccoli;
we saw down tree-like Brussels sprout stems.
We dig for the last carrots, beets, and potatoes
to add to those stored in the barn.
There, they await winter markets and our own winter meals!

Above, in the hayloft,
a mountain of harvested hay bales
stands ready to sell.

The fields rest brown and bare.
Dad tills and plants a cover of oats and rye to protect
and replenish the fields that gave us so much.

Good night, fields, peaceful and still.

Dad cuts back the raspberries
before wind and snow
can crack the canes.

We cart the old brush to burn.
Good-bye to last year's twigs and leaves,
with their bugs and spots!

The promise of
late summer's plump fruit lies
in roots
tucked underground.

Good night, raspberries,
resting below.

We stack wood
by the house and in
the sugarhouse too.
It will heat our home all winter, and
in early spring it will fuel the fire
that boils maple sap into syrup.

Good night, stacked wood, waiting to work!

Before the winter winds come howling
we secure the hoophouse's plastic sides
with ropes
and bales of hay.
Inside,
we float sheets of white cloth
over the baby greens
till the new year's thaw.

Safe under cover
rest little leaves
with mouth-filling names—
spinach, mizuna, tatsoi, arugula.
Our winter salad greens
will nap till stronger sun
can wake them.

Last August the hoophouse grew so hot
        we rolled up the sides and
flung open the doors,
    while picking tomatoes, melons, and
heat-loving okra.

Now, we button up
the perfect shelter for changing weather.

Good night, hoophouse,
wrapped up tight.

We board up chinks in the chicken coop,
and set a timer to give
the hens the light
they need to lay eggs all winter.
We fluff the nests
with hay, plug in the water heater, scoop fresh grain.
We collect the day's eggs,
fragile gifts from our friends.

Good night, chickens, snug in your coop.

With bales of hay we build a windbreak for the beehives
and place a stone on each lid to hold it firm.
We make the hive entrances smaller to keep roaming field mice out.
Within each hive a single queen
lies in a cluster of maids working
to keep her fed.

In September, we harvested honey and wax,
but left enough for the bees
who made enough for us!

Good night, bees, sheltered and safe.

The farmstand is stocked for the holidays
    with fresh eggs, greens and roots,
onions and garlic braids,
    decorative corn,
      honey and maple syrup.
        There's plenty for us and plenty to sell!

Mom and Dad move
planter, cultivator, tiller, and baler
into the equipment shed,
a shelter from rust and cold.
The tractors go in last.

Good night, farm.

The fire jumps in the woodstove.
We feast on homegrown treats—vegetable soup and berry pie.
We pull clinking lights from a box
    untangle tangle
to hang on the porch.

Look! Mom says.

The rising moon,
  the bright sway of stars
  in the sky.

We light beeswax candles
  to soften the longest night.

The farm is ready
for down quilts of snow,
the *shh-shh* of the wind.

Dad tucks us in.

Good night, farmers,
sleep tight.

Sleep tight, farm.

AUTHOR'S NOTE

Every winter, when the farmwork has slowed, I write letters to a neighboring class of third and fourth graders. I write about our chickens, the seeds we are ordering, the growers' meetings we attend, the maple trees we tap, and the plants we start in the greenhouse. The children write back asking questions: *Do you have a dog? Do you like farming? What is your favorite food to grow?*

Then, in May, the children and their wonderful teacher come to the farm for lunch and a visit. They pull weeds, gather eggs, harvest the first strawberries and radishes, and explore the farm. They are such knowledgeable visitors! They know where each food in their lunches comes from. They know that the food they eat at every meal comes from a farm.

They can see that a farm is a lot of work, but for every way that we take care of the farm, it returns the gift—a fresh egg for breakfast, sweet fruit all summer, a place to share and call home all year long.

To the many hands making my work light,
especially those of Sam,
Nora, Silas, and Caleb —E. D.

For David and Hazel —B. S.

Library of Congress Cataloging-in-Publication Data:
Doyle, Eugenie, 1952- author.
Sleep tight farm : a farm prepares for winter / by Eugenie Doyle ; illustrated
by Becca Stadtlander.
pages cm
Summary: It is December, and there are many things for the
family to do around the farm to get it ready for winter.
ISBN 978-1-4521-2901-3 (alk. paper)
1. Farm life—Juvenile fiction. 2. Rural families—Juvenile fiction.
3. Winter—Juvenile fiction. [1. Farm life—Fiction. 2. Family life—Fiction.
3. Winter—Fiction.] I. Stadtlander, Becca, illustrator. II. Title.
PZ7.D7745Man 2015
[E]—dc23
2013043751

JJ
DOYLE
EUGENIE

Nature

10/4

Manufactured in China.

Design by Amelia Mack.
Typeset in Aged.
The illustrations in this book were rendered in paint.

10 9 8 7 6 5 4 3 2 1

Chronicle Books LLC
680 Second Street
San Francisco, California 94107

Chronicle Books—we see things differently.
Become part of our community at www.chroniclekids.com